Miss Bindergarten Gets Ready for Kindergarten

Miss Bindergarten

Gets Ready for Kindergarten

by **JOSEPH SLATE**

illustrated by **ASHLEY WOLFF**

PUFFIN BOOKS

PUFFIN BOOKS
Published by the Penguin Group
Penguin Putnam Books for Young Readers, 345 Hudson Street, New York,
New York 10014, U.S.A.
Penguin Books Ltd, 27 Wrights Lane, London W8 5TZ, England
Penguin Books Australia Ltd, Ringwood, Victoria, Australia
Penguin Books Canada Ltd, 10 Alcorn Avenue, Toronto, Ontario, Canada M4V 3B2
Penguin Books (N.Z.) Ltd, 182-190 Wairau Road, Auckland 10, New Zealand
Penguin Books Ltd, Registered Offices: Harmondsworth, Middlesex, England

First published in the United States of America by Dutton Children's Books,
a member of Penguin Putnam Inc., 1996
Published by Puffin Books, a division of Penguin Putnam Books for Young
Readers, 2001

10 9 8 7 6 5 4

THE LIBRARY OF CONGRESS HAS CATALOGED THE DUTTON EDITION AS FOLLOWS:
Slate, Joseph.
Miss Bindergarten gets ready for kindergarten/by Joseph Slate; illustrated by Ashley Wolff.—1st ed.
p. cm.
Summary: Introduces the letters of the alphabet as Miss Bindergarten and her
students get ready for kindergarten.
ISBN 0-525-45446-2
[1. Alphabet. 2. Animals—Fiction. 3. Kindergarten—Fiction. 4. Schools—Fiction.
5. Stories in rhyme.] 1. Title. PZ8.3.S629Mi 1996 [E]—dc20 96-14692 CIP AC

Puffin Books ISBN 0-14-056273-7

Printed in the United States of America

To Maureen Sheridan Johnson
and all the other Miss Bindergartens,
wherever you are —J.S.

For Margy and Bill,
two of my favorite teachers —A.W.

It is the first day
of kindergarten,
and—
oh, oh, oh!—

Adam Krupp
wakes up.

Brenda Heath
brushes her teeth.

Christopher Beaker
finds
his sneaker.

Miss Bindergarten gets ready for kindergarten.

Danny Hess rushes to dress.

Emily Moko cools her cocoa.

Fran Lister
kisses her sister.

Miss Bindergarten gets ready for kindergarten.

Gwen McGunny
packs her bunny.

Henry Fetter
fights his sweater.

Ian Lowe says, "I won't go!"

Miss Bindergarten gets ready for kindergarten.

Jessie Sike pedals her bike.

Kiki Wong hops along.

Lenny Loome says, "Vroo-vroo-vrooom!"

Miss Bindergarten gets ready for kindergarten.

Matty Lindo
looks out the window.

Miss Bindergarten gets ready for kindergarten.

Patricia Packer
sneaks a cracker.

Quentin Wend
high-fives his friend.

Raffie Mack
high-fives back.

Sara von Hoff
is the first one off.

Miss Bindergarten is *almost* ready

for kindergarten.

Tommy Tuttle jumps a puddle.

Vicky Densel bites her pencil.

Ursula Crewe ties her shoe.

Now Miss Bindergarten is all ready

for kindergarten.

Wanda Chin
marches in.

Xavier Roe
yells
"Hello!"

Yolanda Pound
looks around.

Zach Blair
finds his chair.

"Good morning, kindergarten,"

says Miss Bindergarten.

And—oh, oh, oh!—

the fun's begun!

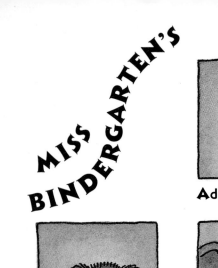

Adam · Alligator

Brenda · Beaver

Christopher · Cat

Danny · Dog

Emily · Elephant

Fran · Frog

Gwen · Gorilla

Henry · Hippopotamus

Ian · Iguana

Jessie · Jaguar

Kiki · Kangaroo

Lenny · Lion

Matty · Moose

Noah · Newt

Ophelia · Otter

Patricia · Pig

Quentin · Quokka

Raffie · Rhinoceros

Sara · Squirrel

Tommy · Tiger

Ursula · Uakari monkey

Vicky · Vole

Wanda · Wolf

Xavier · Xenosaurus

Yolanda · Yak

Zach · Zebra